ROAD TRIP!

A Whiskers Hollow Adventure

STEVE LIGHT

CANDLEWICK PRESS

It was a beautiful day in Whiskers Hollow,
more beautiful than a hubcap shining in the sun.

Bear was out for a drive.

Bear was a good driver—most of the time.

On this day, there was a little accident. *CRASH!*

Bear's old truck needed
a new headlight.

There was only one thing to do.
Bear headed to Rabbit's house.

"Rabbit, let's go—road trip!" called Bear. "I need a new light for my old truck. I need you to help me find one."

"But it's almost lunchtime," said Rabbit.

Rabbit never missed lunch—or breakfast or dinner.

"We'll find a snack along the way," said Bear.

Bear and Rabbit arrived at Mouse's house.

"Mouse, let's go!" called Bear. "Road trip! I need a new light for my old truck, and I need you to help me find one."

"A road trip?" said Mouse. "Oh, I couldn't. Just think what might happen. We could get a flat or run out of gas."

"No need to worry," said Bear kindly. "We'll be together."

Mouse liked being together with Bear and Rabbit. Still, it was scary. But Mouse ran inside to get something—a first-aid kit, because you never know—then hopped into Bear's truck.

The three friends arrived at Donkey's place.

"Let's go—road trip!" said Bear. "I need a new light for my old truck. Can you help us find the way to Elephant's Old Junk Tree?"

Donkey knew the way because Donkey loved junk.

They came to a bridge. It was long and wobbly.

"I don't see any snacks," said Rabbit.

"That looks very rickety," said Mouse.

"Follow me, friends!" called Donkey.

Just down the road, they came to a tunnel.
It was dark and thorny.

"Can't eat thorns," grumbled Rabbit.

"That looks very prickly," said Mouse.

"Follow me, friends!" called Donkey.

Finally they arrived at Elephant's Old Junk Tree. The tree
was filled with old car parts and lots of rusty treasures.
There were tires, tricycles, a guitar with broken strings,
a motorcycle, and lots of wrenches. Even hubcaps!

Bear found some lamps.

Mouse discovered a caution sign.

Donkey dug out a compass.

Rabbit found snacks for everyone.

But they could not find just the right headlight for Bear's old truck.

They were disappointed but decided to enjoy their time together.

Donkey stood up to go. Then the junk started to shift,
and Donkey started to slip!

"Folloooooow meeeee!"

SPLOOSH! They all fell down right into a huge mud puddle!

Bear was covered in thick, gooey mud.

Rabbit stumbled and slid but
held on to the snack.

And Mouse was hopping and skipping—
and having a very good time!

"Help, friend!"
yelled Donkey.

And Elephant knew just what to do.

And there in the mud, they saw it—
the perfect headlight for Bear's old truck.

It was time to go home.

"That was fun!" said Mouse.

"I wouldn't steer you wrong," said Bear.

"And we'll be back in time for dinner," said Rabbit. "Where should we eat?"

"Follow me, friends!" said Donkey.

To friends everywhere

First edition 2021. Library of Congress Catalog Card Number pending. ISBN 978-1-5362-0947-1. This book was typeset in New Century Schoolbook. The illustrations were done in pen and ink and watercolor. Candlewick Press, 99 Dover Street, Somerville, Massachusetts 02144. www.candlewick.com. Printed in Humen, Dongguan, China. 20 21 22 23 24 25 APS 10 9 8 7 6 5 4 3 2